GOOD GIRL, SUNNY PEARL!

Written and Illustrated

By

Ben Wells

ISBN 979-8-9919205-1-3

baw

Books

I dedicate this, my first children's book, to my wife, Jessica, my loving family and friends, and of course the star of the show, our sweet Sunny Pearl!
You have grown to be that precious, angel, long-eared having, blue tick beagle dog that we always knew you had in you!
We love you, sweet Sunny Pearl!

SUNNY PEARL

is a

GIRL

who also is a

DOG

Not a SKUNK

Nor a BEAR

Nor a SHARK

Nor a FROG

She's a

PRECIOUS ANGEL LONG-EARED HAVING BLUE TICK BEAGLE DOG!

HOWEVER!

Sunny Pearl wasn't always a

PRECIOUS

ANGEL

LONG-EARED HAVING

BLUE TICK BEAGLE DOG...

WHO ME?

SHE LOVED TO CHEW
WHAT WASN'T HERS

NO MATTER
WHAT WAS SAID

SHE ATE A PILLOW!

CHEWED A SHOE!

AND EVEN PEED THE BED!

HER

PARENTS

WOULD

SAY...

BAD GIRL, SUNNY PEARL!

She never
LISTENED
when commanded
and
ALWAYS
caused a
RUCKUS

SHE WHIRLED AND TWIRLED AND SWIRLED AND CURLED

JUST LIKE A PUPPY DOG CIRCUS!

HER

PARENTS

WOULD

SAY...

BAD GIRL,

SUNNY PEARL!

SHE ZOOMED IN CIRCLES
UP AND DOWN

AND STAYED UP
PAST HER BEDTIME

SHE JUMPED AND BUMPED AND LUMPED AND SLUMPED...

SHE WAS IMPOSSIBLE TO KEEP IN LINE!

HER PARENTS WOULD SAY...

BAD GIRL,

SUNNY PEARL!

BUT ONE DAY

Sunny Pearl

decided to change!

It was time for

her to become

what she was born to be!

Do you recall?

THAT'S RIGHT!

A PRECIOUS ANGEL LONG-EARED HAVING

BLUE TICK BEAGLE DOG!

She chewed her
BONES
that were her OWN
and went outside
to
POTTY

SHE CALMED HER BARK
AND GAINED A SPARK

AND
SUDDENLY
WASN'T
SO
NAUGHTY!

HER

PARENTS

WOULD

SAY...

GOOD GIRL, SUNNY PEARL!

SHE ACTED RIGHT
AND WOULDN'T FIGHT
WHEN TOLD IT WAS TIME FOR BED

SHE LEFT THE PILLOWS
FOR HER PARENTS

AND CHEWED HER TOYS INSTEAD!

HER PARENTS WOULD SAY...

GOOD GIRL, SUNNY PEARL!

She

LOVED

to

LOVE

and

SNUGGLE

and

HUG

AND BELLY RUBS MADE HER SAY

AHHHHH...

She was proud of

HERSELF

and what she

BECAME

WAIT!
Do you recall?

THAT'S RIGHT!

A

PRECIOUS ANGEL

LONG-EARED HAVING

BLUE TICK

BEAGLE DOG!

AND

HER

PARENTS

SAID...

GOOD GIRL, SUNNY PEARL!

THE END

Milton Keynes UK
Ingram Content Group UK Ltd.
UKHW050811281124
3219UKWH00032B/158
9798991920513